FERAL
TEETH
PRESS

Angels of Anti-Matter

Feral Teeth Press

www.feralteethpress.com

ISBN:9780692697931

First Printing

Cover & Interior Illustrations:
by Mat Fitzsimmons

Angels of Anti-Matter
by Mat Fitzsimmons

ILLUSTRATED

For my brother Pat

Anti-Matter. The opposite of Matter. Those wholesome atoms that bond together to form the nucleus; of all that is, and that will be. I am quite certain that the ancient science of Alchemy, was the pursuit of bending these building blocks, at or to, the whims of the Alchemist. The manipulation of Matter for the benefit of humanity. And while many of these learned men were tried as sorcerers, and hung as wizards, most were sensible, God fearing men; Men that were attempting to alleviate the burdens of mankind, through Science; The mightiest of all the gods. These men believed, and held highest, this Matter, their Science, and all that is good...

Anti-Matter. That dreadful nether-stuff that scientists have now began calling Dark Matter; that scientists are now discovering is so, so, much more abundant than anyone had once thought. Some even theorize that this wholesome good-stuff, Matter, is being suspended like a fly inside amber, floating within the ectoplasmic Anti-Matter. And though this Dark Matter is invisible to the human eye, whether naked or with instrument, scientists *know* that it *does* exist; that it *is* there. The swirling vortices of galaxy swallowing black holes, or, more precisely, those unwholesome building blocks that form those secreted universes; far, far, from the cleansing light of stars, moons, and suns.

As a former practitioner of The Dark Arts, I have traveled, by means of astral locomotion, faster than the speed of *light* into the very heart of a black hole.

There, after a whirlwind visit of 7 nightmare planets built from those unwholesome atoms of Dark Matter, I was finally allowed entrance into the metaphysical realm of that spectral universe; A place whispered to me in hushed tones of the High-Priests of those worlds; The Realm of Spawning Chaos. To be more specific... it was a terrible, *haunted* kingdom, called Gt'rr'U'bhal, a place ruled by one of those fearsome Lords of Outer Darkness... But that is a different tale, told elsewhere—

Upon return from that dream quest, with my mind so nearly shattered, I'd vowed to leave magic, Circle Magic, all of it, firmly in my past. Never again would I attempt to Drift through those vaulted halls of night. I would leave those doors to the nether-realms *closed* for the rest of my days. I would be *done* with my pursuit for the secrets of harnessing black holes and all their malevolent energies; I would be done with *Anti-Matter*!

The thing *was*, Anti-Matter wasn't done with *me*. The Queen of that dreaded place had *tainted* me, no more than a molecule of that stuff from a parallel dimension, but it had been enough. Because of this soiled molecule, which had attached itself to my soul-stuff, the denizens of The Realm of Spawning Chaos have the ability to reach out, to contact me, in the lands of Dream; and they are encouraged to do so by The Lord of Outer Darkness that rules their particular universe. Merely one such universe, in a multiverse much too vast to give such things numbers.

And so, these things from that black-hole-housed universe, seem to visit me with growing frequency; whispering their dread philosophies, preaching religions of madness, and promising gifts from Science, the one god who seems to be even *greater* than The Lords of Outer Darkness. There was a time when the cruelty of Man, evident from any news program on any T.V., had forced me to seek out their philosophies, religions, and scientific breakthroughs... To be nothing like those alchemists of old, harnessing not the power of Matter, but Anti-Matter! Not searching for the secret of gold, but something more like the one that J. Robert Oppenheimer unlocked. To be a necromancer, like a dark Angel of Death!

I try to block out their suggestive ramblings, their insane proposals; these angels. That's how I have now come to think of them, as Angels of Anti-Matter. As I've said, their visits are almost every night now; And to think of these creatures for what I truly fear them to be? Well, that seems as though it would only surely invite madness...So come and have a look. I leave that judgement to you, but, In the words of the Poet, Dante, "Abandon all hope, ye who enters here..."

The first of these night visits that I can recall: A spirit that appeared to be man enough. Through lips sewn shut, he complained that he couldn't get a good sip of coffee. I am addicted to coffee, so I could feel his pain The stiches made it very difficult to understand him, though. I then saw 3 ape-faced ghouls, devouring the flesh of what appeared to be a cadaver, beneath a basilisk the size of an Asian dragon. The man said the corpse had been his wife. She'd killed him when he'd asked her if she would make him some breakfast, then cut out his tongue & ate it with scrambled eggs & home-fries. Now he watches, as the ape-faced ghouls break *their* fast on her bones, breaking her apart piece by piece; Her penance... All of this to the Atomic-Bullfrog-croak-blast of some enormous toad-bat-thing that had appeared in the nebulous ether, there...

Coulrophobic-inducing clowns, incredibly large, come unfolding like huge rubber toys, from a filthy dirty white van. A *Creep* Van; No windows; Side-load door; A faint smell of iron, from so much fluid spilled it will *never, ever* go away. Regardless of *how* much bleach they use. They speak of the first of their kind, in reverential tones, to gain entry into the earthly realm. Satanic Jesters: Bozo, Pogo, & Pennywise. One of these clowns, the one named Raspberry Rot, begrudgingly tells me one of their secrets. In a voice, that sounds as though it had been ground down with a course, metal file, he said: "Remember...Clowns are never laughing *with* you. Clowns are *always* laughing *at* you. The Creep Clowns of the Circus of The Spawning Chaos *always* have the last laugh..." the painted fool giggled & giggled, the sound a sound of madness... His fellow clowns joined in.

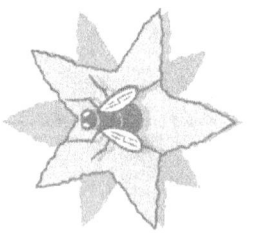

The next of these night spirits, or entities; my *angels...* They brought me to a place beneath cold, black waters; the pressure, nearly more than my soul-stuff could bear. They spoke in watery, modulated voices, chained in straight-jacket-like things at the bottom of this deep, dark aquatic grave. Fat, fanged fish & carrion eating eels, swam amongst these angels, who looked no different than the corpses of drowned sailors, or hydro-therapy victims. when I'd felt as though I was running out of air, felt like the pressure would crush my being like an aluminum can under foot, I asked the angels, "Why have you brought me here?" in a panic... One of the Angels of Anti-Matter answered, amongst a cloud of bubbles, "Because we feed on fear, foolish one, and *all* humans fear death by drowning! Even though it's quite euphoric in comparison to..."

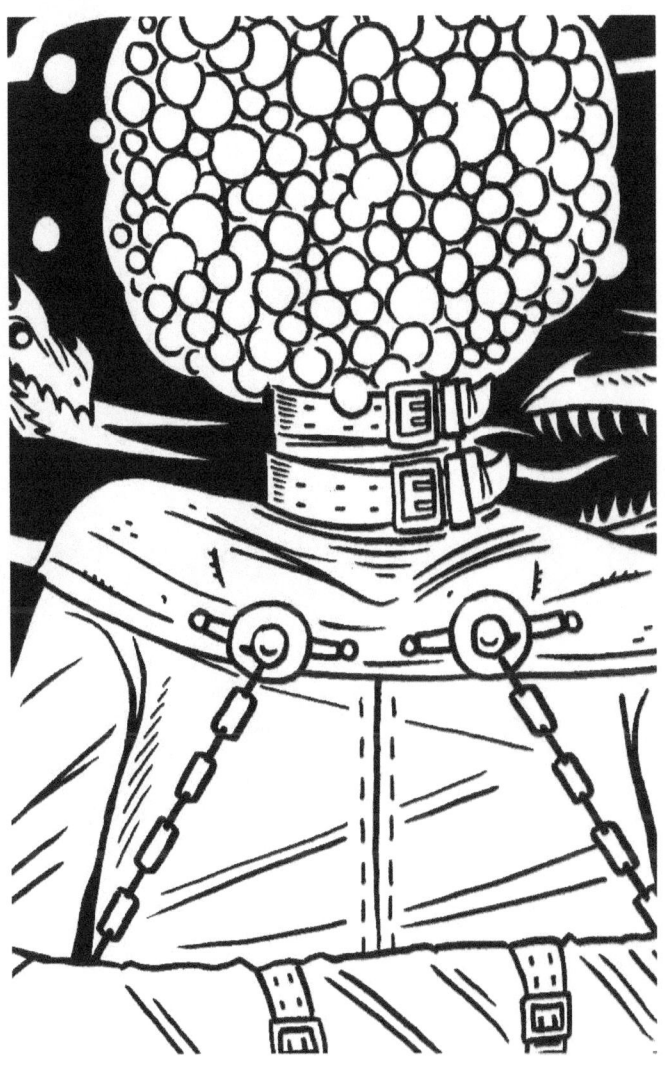

ngels come in varied forms of suppressed terrors & childhood fears; the gathered phobias of the human condition. These particular ones came in the form of a fairytale; A maiden whose soul she has accidently promised to the Devil; His savage lapdog sent to collect her. She, or her soul rather, is bound to this place, The Plain of the Tree of Silence, in chains cuffed behind her back. All is not silent here, though; Skulls, with the dull thunk of bone on bone, swing & knock against one another, macabre wind chimes. Imps, who tend to The Peeling of the Flesh & feed the meat & bones to the great tentacled thing that lives, nameless, below the ground there, laugh from the branches & from the roots of the dead tree. Masks of flayed skin are nailed to the dead tree's trunk. The great man-beast howls, the sound a wretched gurgle; something between wolf & man.

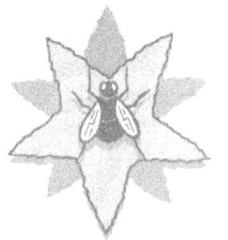

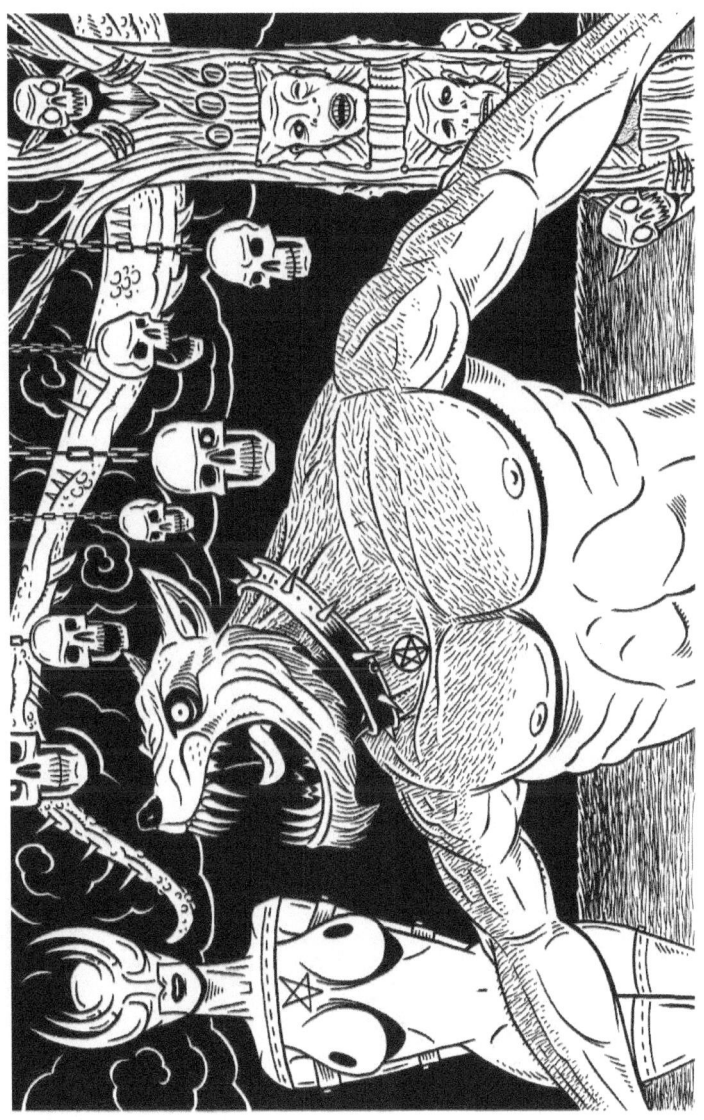

Dental Work. Surgery. Injections, incisions, removals, extractions. Fun stuff, huh? To the person going under the knife, more often than not, an overwhelming fear of the unknown is to be expected. From multi-procedural community funded root-canals, to world-class, sternum-cracking, open-heart explorations; Who wouldn't fear Medicine, the mad twin of Science? Only a fool! Any who have worshiped at Medicine's alter, has more than likely felt the sting of a hypodermic, the slash of the scalpel; Or, perhaps just the bitterness of pill-taste on tongue. These ones, here, tell me that through the miraculous breakthroughs of research, I might one day be like them... I politely tell them that I hope that never happens.

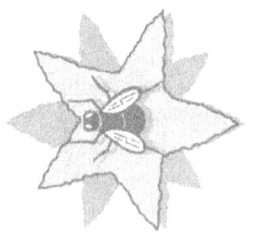

Nights pass, and they, these angels I tell myself, begin to glean ideas of human religion through our interactions. They are most interested in The Book of Revelation, saying they know some of those mentioned there. Behemoth & Leviathan. One Introduces herself to me as Lilith, trying to seduce me with her sex. When I refuse, she brings me before another great overseer in their pantheon, an angel named Asmodeus. In The Realm of the Spawning Chaos, His virtue is that of Lechery, and *here* his virtue can be seen far & wide. A man in street clothes is being devoured head first by some kind of crawling monstrosity. I feel like some polar opposite version of William Blake! Another angel, smiling, with a head & face of blistering meat, is about to be consumed by spiders...

Demonical sultans, were those 2 who had set up their strongholds within the shadow of the cyclopean wall of Gt'rr'U'bhal. And it was they who came to court me next. These 2 were mighty conspirators with the Queen of the realm, she whose name was *never* to be spoken out loud. The first of these sultans looked nearly human, with exception to his massive size—*twice* that of the *tallest* man of Earth—along with his horrible ogre's teeth. The giant wore the skin of another demon, or angel, rather; Perhaps the trophy of some tooth & nail brawl, in this universe devoid of love. The other sultan is even more of a brute. It is *that* one that confronts me, angrily, "Go away meddling little human. You've interrupted our fucking, and we have no secrets here!" The brute shook his manhood at me, which was the size of my arm. "This is our harem, and *these*, our concubines, would grind you to *dust*, boy! *So*, GO!"

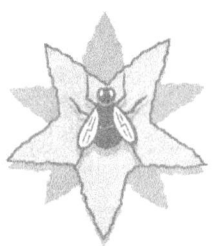

When I am visited by these angels, these creatures projecting themselves & their surroundings into my sleeping brain, they no longer even *try* to disguise their true nature, anymore. Yes, many of them have clear, bi-lateral symmetry, but they are *far* from what we on Earth could ever consider human. As the time goes moving by, night after night, I grow less inclined to think of these things, my Angels of Anti-Matter, as angels, at all anymore. They now scare me; there is nothing in this place that is visible in the darkness. Not even weak flickering flames, of ghost-lit candles, winking out from streaked dirty windows. No, not even that. These creatures are self-illuminating, like some fish that swim at the bottom of the dark sea...

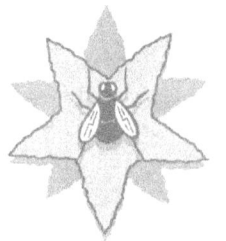

Sinners of the highest order they are, these ones here; Part of an inner circle, like secret police, to the Queen of The Realm of Spawning Chaos, herself. They are what would be the exact opposite of divine, whatever that may be. Unholy? But, they are here to mete out justice, just the same; the more painful the punishment, the better! These ones are not squeamish. There's a man on our Earth who knows the name of these creature's Guild; Their Order. An Order most adept in the Arts of Torment & Suffering. You'll find the name of their secret Order in the work of a Mr. Barker... and I will speak no more of them here.

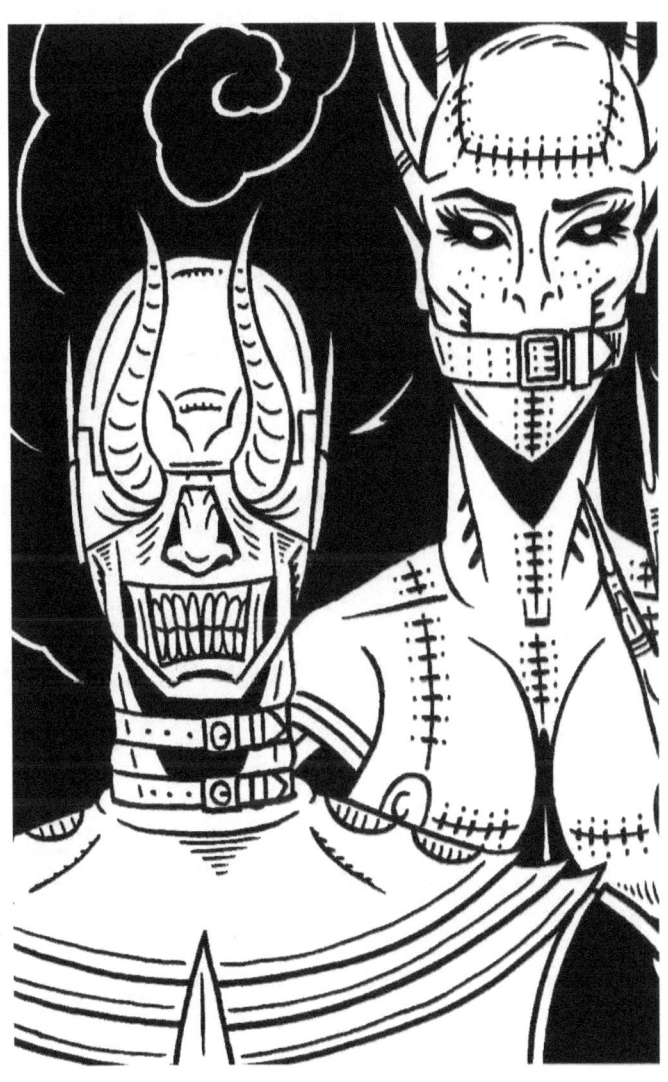

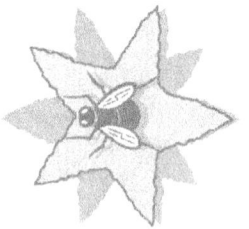

Encircled by a wall of black flame, like Johnny Cash... Only I didn't fall into this burning ring of fire; I was pulled here. Pulled by those spectral entities, who began as simple phobias & childish terrors; Who now show themselves for what they truly are: Servitors to those dread forces, The Lords of Outer Darkness. They've evolved. In this ring of fire, an archetypical devil, Mammon is his name, showed me all I had to lose. Again, Mammon offered me intercourse with a demoness who happened to be there; 6 breasted, with legs that terminated into the hoofs of a goat. Again, I declined this offer. Mammon pointed past the demoness harlot, pointing to a man whose head was wreathed in flames; an enormous Hellhound, pulling at strands of his intestines, as if some Promethean Eagle. A thing, some Baby-Huey version of The Bat Boy, hung like John Holmes, stood there sizing me up; I cared not to think for what... "That could be you," Mammon said, still pointing at the man being eaten by the hound.

A pageant. A procession. A parade. These ones, swinging censers that emit a foul & repugnant odor, sing a liturgy to the Dark Matter. In this realm, it was this mysterious & darksome stuff, that had once given birth to The Lords of Outer Darkness, at the beginning of time. They would not sing the Queen's name. Not in this dimension, for she was so very near. She was not on this planet, that I was Drifting on now, but one close by. I heard the names of some of those other strange, terrible, lords in their hymn, though. Nyarlathotep, Xushathula, and Shubb-Niggurath. There words were like gunshots at close range, upon my ears. The one like a shadowed he-goat, kept an insane marching beat with his stomping hooves, as the lesser minions climbed over The Anti-Pope. He continued his sermon, preaching the merits of absolute malice, as soldiers grunted & growled, slavering & anxious to do battle—

Fungus, wet & hot. The humidity here is like nothing on our good green Earth. This place has the smell of decaying swamp & the heat of Vulcan's furnace. Something growing from a great stalk blows a trumpet, the sound causing a disturbance in atmosphere. Another angel flies through the air on its dragonflies' wings; a tumorous mass, with the arms of a man & a Kabuki-mask type head perched upon a serpentine neck; though it is *not* wearing a mask. There is a creature with no eyes, and an erection, ending in a bone dagger; a sure promise of pain & agony for some poor unfortunate soul. Besides the hopping, tittering little shadows jumping around on mushroom caps, there's a weird pig-bat-fish-bug thing, Another eyeless serpent type monstrosity with the mouth of a lamprey, along with a buzzard-headed bird-man. All of these creatures seem to be fleeing something, like the animals in *'Watership Down'*... Something apparently coming my way—

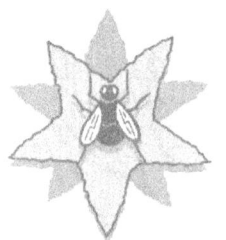

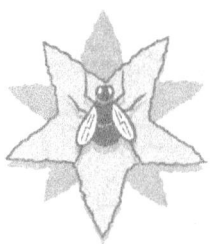

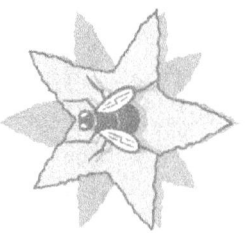

reat dust storms have been recorded on film, in the Plains of the American Mid-West & bone-bleaching desert of Egypt; towering walls of black dirt, or sand, reaching high enough to block out the sun! That was what the thing storming down upon me now, was like, if a dust storm were given the head of a bull – wearing a nose-ring, decorated with the skull of some alien giant—then blazing liquid flames, streaming like Greek Fire, from its gaping nostrils. I was dwarfed by the stygian bull, surely some great Duke of these hidden, lurking dimensions. Sure that my soul-stuff would be flattened, trampled under hoof, the psychic residue cremated in the terrible beast's wake; I reached out, telepathically, to anything wholesome that might be wandering this particular black hole; Anything that may be able to intervene & save my soul-stuff, which really, was the essence of everything I am.

Oh has one ever been so happy to be favored by, if not the *gods*, at least *a* god! As I was certain of my soul-stuff's demise (which would be death in *all* the realms of the multiverse), the roaring of a billion stampeding hooves, the rotten hurricane-force wind trying to tear me to shreds; Suddenly! I heard the keening sound of what seemed to be myriad ripping radial-saws, mixed with the magnified metallic wail of a sharpening stone's wheel. Looking up, I saw a vessel, its iron-clad hull various hues of dull alien greens, and greys. Something from science-fiction, back on Earth. A starship! The angles were more drawn out & it was many times larger, but it was not dissimilar to a stealth bomber; just more exotic, more alien in its build & appearance. At the moment that I was sure imminent death was upon me, I was pulled apart by a bright, healthy, beam of light. Before I realized what had hit me, I was standing on a metallic deck, the deck of the starship, re-materialized! The entire vessel was made of a transparent steel, but, like a one-way mirror. I hadn't seen anything except for metal, while I'd been standing on the plain down below. A strange woman, with a strange owl perched on her shoulder, stepped forward introducing herself. "I've been keeping a watchful eye on you, brave little mortal," she was an Amazon, a Valkyrie, a giant's daughter, "it is not just anyone who wanders into the nether-realms of Anti-Matter. I am Pallas. Pallas Athena... I heard your call."

145

Illustrator/ author Mat Fitzimmons lives in Santa Cruz, California, with his wife Brandi & voluptuous kitty Chloe. Mr. Fitzsimmons enjoys aquatic activities, reading weird fiction, flipping through illustrated books, and collecting Japanese monster & robot toys. He's also been known to front the hyper-aggro-garage-rock monsters; Herbert; and, Automatic Animal (albums available on iTunes), now & again. This is Mr. Fitzsimmons' 3rd book project with Feral Teeth Press, with several upcoming projects in the works...

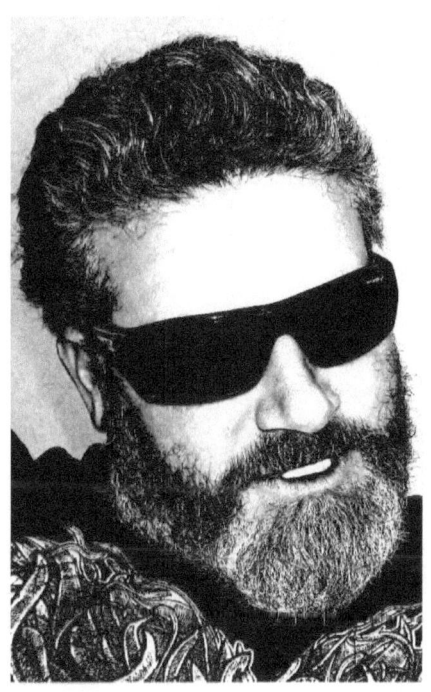

De Mysteriis Ex Ultra

BY MAT FITZSIMMONS

NOW AVAILABLE!!!
An Illustrated Dream-Quest
136 Pages

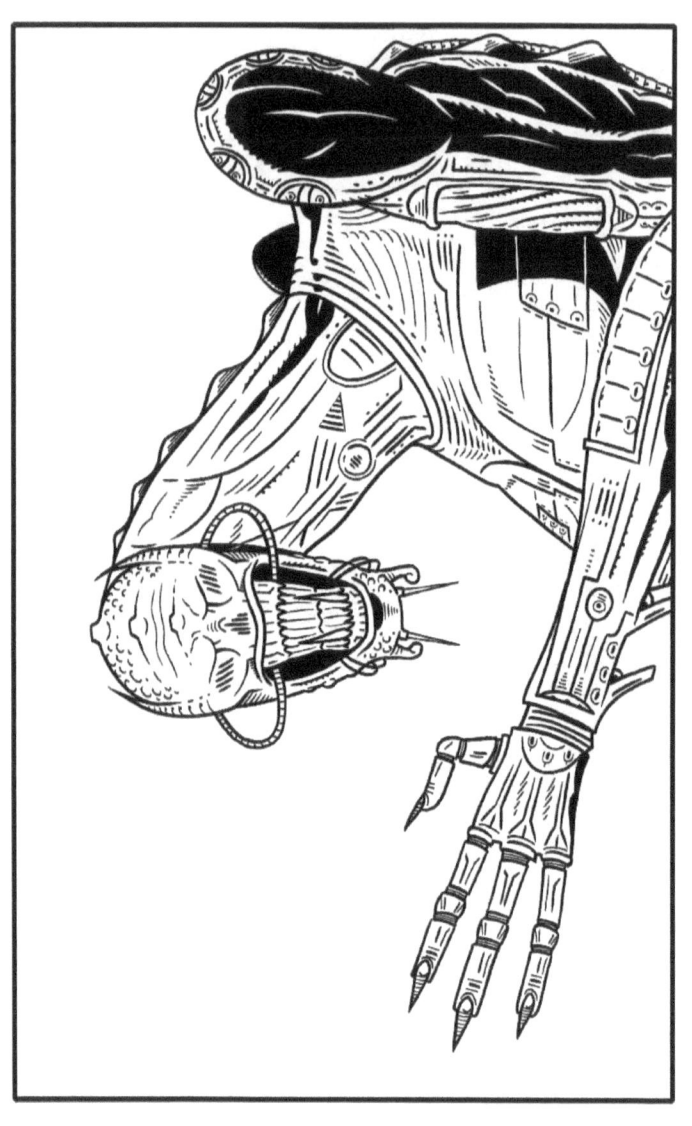